Written by Emily Gale

Illustrations and cover design by
Joëlle Dreidemy

With special thanks to
Justine Smith and Hannah Cohen

First published in Great Britain in 2014 by Buster Books,
an imprint of Michael O'Mara Books Limited,
9 Lion Yard, Tremadoc Road, London SW4 7NQ

 www.mombooks.com/buster

 Buster Books

 @BusterBooks

A CIP catalogue record for this book is available from the British Library.

ISBN: 978–1–78055–170–8

10 9 8 7 6 5 4 3

Printed and bound in April 2019 by CPI Group (UK) Ltd, 108 Beddington Lane,
Croydon, CR0 4YY, United Kingdom.

Papers used by Michael O'Mara Books are natural, recyclable products
made from wood grown in sustainable forests. The manufacturing processes
conform to the environmental regulations of the country of origin.

Eliza BOOM'S Diary

My Explosive Adventure

BUSTER

TOP SECRET!

↘

THIS DIARY BELONGS TO

Eliza Boom

SATURDAY NIGHT
My Lab, 7pm

Dear Diary,

We've been banished to the lab, for ever.

You'll understand why when I tell you about my

latest invention.

That's me, Eliza

That's my dog, Einstein

It was Invention 92: The Super-Sneaky
Spy-Cam Collar.

Invention 92
(modelled by
Einstein)

Shiny!

Useful!

Brilliant!

This is what happened to it.

Don't worry, Einstein wasn't wearing it at the time.

Dad says that before every good invention there are 99 not-so-good ones. That was number 92. I'm SO close, Diary.

Everyone in my family had the grumps after the explosion.

Not again, Eliza!

Alice, my step-mum (super-cross, as usual)

Dad (cross)

Plum, my baby sister (cross, b still cute)

8

Einstein is the only one who has forgiven me.

He understands me even if no one else does.

This is him.

My best friend

He loves wearing his lab coat.
Seriously, he does.

I named him Einstein after the real Einstein who was a scientist. But he's dead now. Not my dog, the scientist.

Do you know what hurt the most?

It was what Dad said:

Go to your bedroom this instant, Eliza!

He knows I don't have a bedroom. I have a lab.
Bedrooms are just for sleeping in. I'm too busy
inventing to sleep!

Dad has a lab too, only his is disguised as a garden shed.

Never judge a shed by its cover.

Dad is a fully qualified inventor who makes gadgets for spies, and I'm his assistant. I like being an assistant inventor but one day I'd actually like to be a SpY, too. I mean, why should someone else get to have all the fun with mY inventions?

Speaking of inventions, how did my Super-Sneaky Spy-Cam Collar go so wrong? It would have been perfect for tracking down where Einstein buries our things ...

Me, inventing The Super-Sneaky Spy-Cam Collar

... like Alice's shoes,

... Plum's toys,

... and even Dad's tools

from his tool belt.

I showed Alice my super invention yesterday before it exploded. She should have been super-impressed, but she barely looked at it. That was very non-super of her.

No one cares about any of my inventions — especially Alice. All she cares about is her garden. That's why she confiscated Invention 91: The Spy Rocket, that I invented last week. She just doesn't understand me or my inventions.

Alice, Chief Inventor of A Boring Rose Bush

Invention 91 (crashed)

My plan was to make Einstein wear his Super-Sneaky Spy-Cam Collar and then I'd watch the film to see where his secret stash was buried.

But when I connected The Super-Sneaky Spy-Cam to the telecommunication system (the TV) via the electric current carrier (the TV cable), and put on our flying particle protectors (goggles) ... well, you know what happened:

And that brings us back to right now.

I'm desperate to come up with an even better invention. That's why we're upside-down — it helps you think. It also makes your hair grow, which is probably why we both have big, fuzzy hairstyles.

Thinking ... thinking ... I just know something will come to me soon.

Yours inventively,
Eliza Boom
Inventor-in-Training

P.S. As I'm writing my inventions in your pages, Diary, you should have a scientific name, too.

I name this diary "Edison".

Edison invented this:

That's a lightbulb, by the way, not a worm

SUNDAY NIGHT
My Lab, 9pm ← *Busy day!*

Dear Edison,

All that thinking has led to my new invention:
Diva-Pro Ultra-Heated Hair Rollers.

Invention 93,
please prove Dad
wrong and WORK!

↙

Hair this wild needs SCIENCE.

Everything was going to plan until ...

MINI BOOM!

... our rollers exploded and Einstein ran away.

I quickly took my rollers out and went looking for him. In the hallway I caught sight of my hair.

I looked more like a Golden Retriever than a Super-Cool Diva!

Woof?

Using hairclips, I performed vital emergency surgery and soon the search for Einstein was back on ...

... which led me to Dad's shed.

When I got inside things did **not** look good.

Dad was crying and trying to tear out his hair.
Which is hard to do when you're already bald.

There seemed to be a problem with Dad's amazing MindReader2000.

It wasn't reading minds. This was serious! Without reading minds The MindReader2000 was just a very ugly hat.

By now, Dad had done so much crying he had hiccups. Being an inventor is very stressful.

Dad needed urgent help, and I was it.

BOOM!

First, I got rid of his hiccups.

Then I had a good look at The MindReader2000. Fortunately I had my tool belt and head torch with me.

Straight away I spotted the problem — a loose screw in a tiny hole. I was going to need a very special tool to remove it ...

The hairclip

Happy Dad

a hairclip!

Easy. Peasy.

Dad was grateful, but instead of asking me to help some more he said I had to go.

SUSPICIOUS!

Why was he in such a hurry to get rid of me? It was time to do some spying of my own.

I scratched a peephole in the blacked-out window of his shed.

Dad was at his computer. There was a shadowy figure on the screen. It must have been Dad's Spy Boss, the one in charge of all the spies. The voice coming out was low and rumbly like a robot running out of battery. I could only make out two words:

MISSION ... METALLIC

Suddenly, Einstein appeared at my side and we had to make a getaway before Dad caught us.

We ran straight back to my lab and I removed Einstein's Diva-Pro rollers.

He was very upset by the results. Sorry, my
furry friend. I had to spend the rest of the
night comforting him.

He wanted a never-ending tummy rub. But I had
work to do if I was going to figure out how to
get Dad to take me seriously as an inventor and
introduce me to his Spy Boss.

So I invented something that would occupy Einstein:

Invention 94:
The Never-Ending
Tummy Rubber
(please work so
I can show Dad!)

Yours inventively,
Eliza Boom
Assistant Inventor

P.S. I can't stop thinking about

MISSION METALLIC ...

MONDAY MORNING
My Lab, 7am

Dear Edison,

Good news: as Einstein snored next to me,
I woke up at 4am with an invention buzzing
around my head.

It was a present for Dad to make sure he never has trouble with tiny screws messing up his genius machines.

METHOD:

Glue five super-strong magnets on to one of Alice's pink washing-up gloves (thanks, Alice).

Invention 95

Super-strong magnets

And there you have it ... The Magno-Glove!

Testing inventions is really important. The sun wasn't up yet but I couldn't wait. I tiptoed round the house wearing The Magno-Glove.

Teaspoon

Screw

Fork

It was going brilliantly until ...

... I accidentally woke up Plum. Her screeching made Einstein start to howl ...

... which woke up the rest of the house.

That's when Alice busted me.

Eliza Boom, is that my washing-up glove? Hand it over to me, young lady.

There was only one way those magnets were coming off. **SNIP!** Well, I couldn't give away my super-powerful magnets, could I?

This is what the glove looked like when I gave it back ...

... Alice will have to do the washing-up with one hand!

Dad sent everyone back to bed, but I couldn't sleep.

I lay awake thinking about school, and how much easier my life would be if Zoe Wakefield was nicer.

ZOE WAKEFIELD, Class Meanie

Mean Mouth Machine (where all her horrible comments come out)

Perfect hair, of course

Heart made of stone

The more I thought about Zoe, the more knotted my tummy became. I get that way after I've eaten dairy, too.

Super-Allergy Sundae

My allergies:
1. Dairy (especially ice cream)
2. Horses (itchy blotches and sneezing)
3. Einstein (sometimes dog hair gives me a rash — but he's worth it)

And finally, the worst allergy of all,

4. Zoe Wakefield, Queen of Mean.

Zoe being mean to me isn't new. But she's having a party this week and I CAN'T be the only kid not invited.

Don't worry, Edison, I've got a plan: what if I give Zoe a present before her birthday? She'll have to invite me then! And what if it's something as amazing as this?

A STAR IN A JAR!

Invention 96

STEP 1:

Take one jar.

STEP 2:

Measure and cut some

fishing wire.

STEP 3:

Tie a beautiful star

to one end.

STEP 4:

Stick the fishing wire to

the inside of the lid with

a super-strong magnet.

It's impossible to look at

it and not say,

"*ooooh*".

I wrapped the jar in some home-made wrapping paper, but it still didn't look pretty enough. Luckily I had some cool black, stripey ribbon that I found last week in Alice's flower beds.

Einstein thinks it's pretty!

I just know I'm going to win Zoe's heart with this invention, and get an invitation to her party.

Sorry Edison, I've got to go. Alice is shouting, "School time!" It's always "Something-Time" with Alice.

Before I go, here's how we look after being up all night inventing

Yours inventively,
Eliza Boom
24-Hour Inventor

MONDAY AFTERNOON
My Lab, 5pm

Dear Edison,

Bad news! When I got to school I found out that everyone in my class had the same idea about a pre-birthday birthday present for Zoe.

Zoe made us line up so she could inspect the presents. It was so embarrassing.

It was like being at an audition in front of the world's most evil judge. Nobody's present was good enough for Zoe.

It was my turn next.

I held my breath as Zoe took off the ribbon and unwrapped the jar.

This is what she said:

My daddy named a REAL star after me when I was five. It's bigger than the sun. Loser!

AAAAAAAARGHHHHHHH!

She hated my invention. It was a disaster.

So I asked Zoe for the jar back, and the weird ribbon that I'd found in Alice's flower beds (I knew Einstein would appreciate it!), but Zoe had other ideas.

She took the ribbon and tied it into her perfect hair and put the jar in her bag.

Wow, did that mean she was going to invite me to her party after all?

Zoe sat down to write down the names of all the kids she was inviting and then all the kids not invited.

She stuck the list on the wall and left the classroom, chucking my beautiful, handmade wrapping paper in the bin as she went.

Everyone rushed over to find their name.

INVITED

Almost the entire
human race

NOT
INVITED

Eliza Boom

Amy Madden,
A.K.A. Mayo-Amy

What's so wrong with me and Mayo-Amy?
Amy's new this year. I hardly know her (I'm
usually too busy inventing to make friends). But
I do know that Amy's mum washed her hair in
MAYONNAISE to get rid of nits.

Poor Amy: her
mum thought she
was a salad

Everyone says she
smells eggy. That's
probably why she's
not invited either.

As for me, what a waste of a good invention!

Now Zoe has one of my super-strong magnets, and it was all for nothing. I felt just like the scrunched-up wrapping paper she'd thrown in the bin.

I came home to more disaster. Dad was pulling the place apart, looking for something.

50

Poor Dad. He'd fitted his new invention with a tracking device, but that had gone missing, too!

Einstein promised he hadn't buried it, and what else could I do but believe him? After all, he is my best friend.

Who could resist this face?

Dad looked everywhere, and I helped.

Then Plum waddled in, dressed like a tiger, with a very long, stripey tail.

Dad grabbed Plum by the tail.

It's long and black and stripey like this! Only it's actually a piece of **metallic ribbon** and contains *Top-Secret Spy Information!* Anyone seen it? AAANNNYYYONE?

Oh, Edison! That's when I realized! And ran to my lab to hide under the duvet, where I plan to stay, minding my own business for the rest of my life. Don't ask me why, Edison.

Just don't!

Fine, you win! I'll tell you.

The ribbon I used on Zoe's present isn't ribbon at all. Remember how I said I found it in Alice's flower beds? And remember how strange it was? That's because it isn't ribbon — it's Dad's invention!

The Mission Metallic Info-Ribbon

So all those secret spy messages ... are in ZOE WAKEFIELD'S HAIR!

Dad could lose his job over this! Which means I would lose mine!

Edison, somehow, despite my best intentions and brilliant inventions, I've created:

AN INTERNATIONAL EMERGENCY

So, I've decided I can't hide in my lab.

I'll go to school tomorrow and demand the ribbon back from Zoe.

Dad needs me. The world needs me!

Yours guiltily,
Eliza Boom
Inventor-in-Trouble

TUESDAY NIGHT
My Lab, 7pm

Dear Edison,

As soon as I got to school, I pleaded with Zoe

to give the ribbon back.

Only if you say:
"Please, please, please
Zoe, you are awesome
and I, Eliza Boom, am
a L.O.S.E.R."

And she wasn't even joking. I had to make myself picture Dad last night in utter despair just so I could get the words out. But I did it, Edison. And then she said ...

NO.

I was so angry I thought my eyeballs would pop out of my face.

I felt someone's hand give my shoulder a gentle squeeze. It was Mayo-Amy. That made me feel a tiny bit better, but then I thought I was going to cry so I ran out of the classroom.

I went to my special thinking place:

Eliza Boom in her natural habitat: the school science cupboard

I had to pretend Einstein was with me. I think better with him around

I had to make my brain work extra-hard to figure out how to get the ribbon back.

My extra-hard-working brain

Thinking ...

Thinking ...

There is so much useful stuff for junior inventors in that cupboard. It was giving me ideas just looking at all of those tubes and clips and things. I thought: if I borrow them and bring them back later, I might be able to ...

... Save the world! Plus Dad!

Good old brain. In a flash it came up with

Invention 97.

This is
Invention 97:
The Grabber

I stuffed my new invention down the back of

my shirt and hurried to class.

I was really late!

Ms Bacon did not
look happy

But that was the least of my worries, because
the next thing I knew ...

I was flying!

When I crash-landed, I looked back to see
Zoe's gigantic foot in the way.

She had tripped me up!

The worst part was that The Grabber had fallen
out, and Ms Bacon didn't believe my story about
borrowing school equipment to save humankind.

So I'd lost The Grabber and I was off to see Principal Bixley. I'm scared of Principal Bixley. She always smells of cheese and you know how I get around dairy.

Sit there and think about your actions, Eliza Boom.

I did exactly as I was told. I sat there and thought about what actions I needed to take to get that ribbon off Zoe Wakefield's horrible head.

At home-time, the weirdest thing happened.

I was standing with Mayo-Amy when Zoe Wakefield ... SMILED at us.

I've decided you can both come to my party after all. It's fancy dress and whoever wins best costume gets to take home whatever they want.

Then she twiddled the ribbon and winked at me.

"Whatever they want ..." BRILLIANT! All I've got to do is invent the best costume and I'll ask for the 'ribbon' back. (If I tell Zoe it's a brilliant invention, she'll never let me have it!)

Yours inventively,
Eliza Boom
Costume-Inventor Extraordinaire

64

TUESDAY NIGHT
Still in the Lab, 9.30pm

Dear Edison,

The BAD NEWS is ...

I asked Dad just how much trouble we'd be in if we never got the ribbon back.

He couldn't even speak. He just croaked a bit and held out his arms as wide as he could.

The GOOD NEWS is ...

I've designed a costume so amazing that the next time I see Dad I'll be making him the happiest inventor alive.

Invention 98:
The Cave
of Fireflies

Newspaper
and paste

Christmas lights
and black paint

Papier-mâché + electronic genius = I'M A CAVE
... OF FIREFLIES!

Einstein loves it so
much he's going to
sleep in it all night.

I'm sure my sparkly cave invention will win

best costume.

Yours hopefully,
Eliza Boom
Inventerrific!

WEDNESDAY NIGHT
My Lab, 8.30pm

Dear Edison,

I'm back from Zoe Wakefield's party, feeling just like Cinderella when she got home from the ball.

It's no use, Edison, I can't lie to you. Actually, I feel **NOTHING LIKE CINDERELLA.**

The main difference is that Cinderella turned up in a beautiful dress and the crowd gasped.

Cinderella

GASP!

Whereas I, Eliza Boom, turned up as a cave, while poor Mayo-Amy turned up as a dog, and everyone LAUGHED. Because it wasn't a costume party after all!

Zoe, you said it was fancy dress?!

You must have heard me wrong because of your weird ear-muff hair, hahahahaha!

I was upset but I had to pull myself together.
Zoe had Dad's secret spy ribbon in her hair and
I wasn't leaving until I had it back.

Zoe's mum helped me take off the cave so I could
join in the 'special activity' they had planned.

I noticed Mayo-Amy checking the costume out.
She looked impressed, but I tried not to let that
distract me.

It was time for the 'special activity'.

Mrs Wakefield told everyone to go out into the garden.

I followed Zoe, wondering what the 'special activity' could be ...

This was it. Horses, why did it have to be horses?

My worst
nightmare

Zoe told us the horses' names: Dancer, Prancer, Frisky, Mary and Daisy.

Inside my head I quickly renamed them all:
Danger, Double-Danger, Risky, Scary and Crazy.

There was a big, hairy horse lady standing in front of those evil snorting beasts.

She looked like she ate horses for breakfast!

Zoe got on the
white one: Dancer,
A.K.A. Danger.

She made us wait ages while she picked riders
for the other horses.

Unlike the other kids, Mayo-Amy was trying
to hide. I started to think we had a few things
in common.

Of course, I didn't need to hide because Zoe
would never pick me for anything.

I think Zoe's next words were:

Eliza, I pick you to ride Daisy.

But this is what I heard:

Eliza, say goodbye to this world. You're about to be galloped to your very itchy **DEATH!**

Edison, She picked me! Zoe knew about my allergies and my very real fear of horses. What happened next is too horrible to talk about.

But I will.

The hairy horse lady picked me up and put me on to Crazy-Daisy, whose tail was swishing like it hated me already.

I started to itch.

But when I tried to tell the hairy horse lady about my allergy, she didn't seem to hear me. She was staring at Zoe's hair.

First we walked around a bit. I think we did anyway, I had my eyes closed.

Then I heard Zoe say "FASTER!", and just like everyone else on the planet, the horses obeyed her.

"Trot!"

Trotting was horrible. It felt like a punishment! Maybe I deserved one for giving Zoe the spy ribbon and getting Dad into trouble.

Meanwhile, Zoe was showing off and that's when I saw my chance.

I shimmied up my horse's neck and reached out to get a bit closer ... closer ... CLOSER ...

Nearly there!

... but then I got distracted by the hairy horse lady, who *still* seemed interested in Zoe's ribbon too, and ...

... all I remember next is seeing Zoe's face in the sky, the ribbon Still in her hair, and me landing like this:

THUD!

The next party activity was a bouncy castle, but
I was still feeling bruised from my fall. I stayed
in the kitchen and watched the food coming out.

The cake was a huge pink
castle with a girl made
of marzipan who looked
exactly like Zoe.

I picked up some tongs from the table and
thought about knocking the head right off that
mean marzipan girl.

But that's when a plan came to me. I'd tong the
ribbon out of Zoe's hair while she was blowing
out her candles!

With everyone back inside
ready for cake, and a
tea towel draped over my
arm to conceal the tongs,
my new plan was working ...

... until Zoe said:

Mummy, don't forget the
special dessert for Eliza.
She's allergic to cake.

I dropped the tongs!

Before I knew it, I was face-to-face with
another of my nightmares.

ICE CREAM.

The Deathly Dairy,
with sprinkles

Mrs Wakefield seemed so nice — how could I tell
her that ice cream makes me puke?

You think this diary entry will end in misery, Edison, but you're wrong. A surprise Someone came to my rescue.

Mayo-Amy!

She grabbed the spoon and saved me before my very eyes.

And that's when I realized that Mayo-Amy had to be part of my next plan.

The plan had two parts:

1. Stop calling Mayo-Amy 'Mayo-Amy'. Even though it's only in my head.

2. Ask Amy to be my new assistant. Assistant of the Assistant to the Inventor for International Espionage (that means spying). AAIIE for short.

I told Amy about the plan. She thought about part two of the plan for a moment and then said:

You need an assistant and I need a best friend. Deal?

Yes, you read that right Edison ... she wants to be my friend, too. Yay!

Before we left the party, I told Amy all about the spy ribbon containing secret information.

She was shocked. She's coming to my house before school tomorrow to help me invent a new gadget to get the ribbon back for real this time.

I'm excited, Edison! But now I have to lie down. I'm aching all over after that death-defying ride on Crazy-Daisy.

Yours, covered in bruises,
Eliza Boom
Assistant Inventor
(who also has an assistant!)

Frozen peas

THURSDAY NIGHT
My Lab, 7pm

Dear Edison,

Amy was here by 7am. I love how dedicated she is.

First I introduced her to Einstein. They're going to get on really well ...

Amy loves dogs!

It turns out that Amy and I have loads more
in common.

Amy is terrified of horses, too.
And she has an allergy. Pineapples.

Killer Pineapple

Killer Horse

Our new idea is really one of my old ideas, only much better.

Invention 99:
THE SUPER-FLEXI PERISCOOP
(a new and improved Grabber)

We wrote out our plan in proper spy-speak.

The Plan:

Locate 'Enemy 1' (Zoe!)

Camouflage special agents (hide!)

Assemble hardware
(aim The Super-Flexi Periscoop!)

Identify cargo (check she's wearing the ribbon!)

Activate weapon (grab the ribbon!)

Evacuate scene (run!)

We raided the kitchen and Dad's lab for extra supplies in case we needed to invent something on-the-go.

Then we changed into special spy kit, and tried to carry as many of my inventions as we could, including The Diva-Pro Hair Rollers (you never know), and the washing-up glove fingers with super-strong magnets on (left over from The Magno-Glove).

Super-Shades for
Super-Spies →

Before we left for school, Amy and I said goodbye to Einstein who was feeling sad about being left behind.

Poor Einy ...

So I gave him one of Alice's shoes as a special treat (it's okay, he'd already buried the other one so it was no good to Alice any more).

All the kids were out in the playground before school started. We were in a perfect position ...

... until BRRRRRRRR! The school bell rang – five minutes early!

ALL STUDENTS
TO THE MAIN HALL
FOR FULL INSPECTION!

We'd never had a *full* inspection before.
No one knew what it could mean. What
were they looking for? Nits? Chickenpox?
Lipstick? Lollies?

All Amy and I cared about was that it was
interrupting our plan.

In the hall, Principal Bixley came on stage.

Straight away I noticed what everyone else seemed to have missed (I was born to be a spy):

It wasn't the REAL Principal Bixley! For a start she was giant-sized, with a beard.

That's when it hit me, Edison. The hairy horse lady from Zoe's party and this principal were the same person! A HOSTILE INFILTRATOR as we say in the spy trade.

Real principal

Hairy horse lady

Phony principal

Then, Fake
Principal
Bixley made an
announcement:

Owing to a health and safety issue,
pupils will have to remove all hair items
immediately. Hair bands,
hair ties, hairclips, hair elastics,
hair bobbins, and any other hair
hardware. Especially hair ribbons.
Move it!

The room went wild. I nudged Amy and waited
for her to see that this was all a trick ...

It didn't take her long to figure it out. The trouble was we didn't know what to do next.

Zoe Wakefield was having a tantrum about how long she'd spent doing her hair that morning. WITH MY SPY RIBBON, OF COURSE!

I won't take it out! I won't, I won't, I won't! This perfect hair took me three hours!

Three hours? I couldn't help wondering if Zoe styled her hair with her feet — why else would it take that long?

Despite Zoe's tantrum, the spy ribbon went into a huge bag that was being passed around. Soon after, the bag and Fake Principal Bixley had DISAPPEARED!

We were being outsmarted! I didn't like it one bit. So I took Amy to my special thinking place.

But when we arrived at the science cupboard, it was locked!

We could hear teachers banging on the door from the inside.

This is Eliza Boom and Amy Madden. Don't panic, we're going to get you out of there.

BANG! BANG!

Then I heard the Real Principal Bixley's voice through the door.

Eliza Boom! Do not use explosives! I repeat, NO EXPLOSIVES!

That did it. If Real Principal Bixley was going to bring up things from the past, I'd leave her in there and continue on the hunt for Fake Principal Bixley (F.P.B.).

We had to find F.P.B. before the spy ribbon was gone for good. We set off right away.

On the way, I had an idea. Dad had told me his spy ribbon invention was metallic. What if I used one of the super-strong magnets from Invention 95, formerly known as The Magno-Glove?

You could dangle a magnet into the F.P.B.'s bag with The Super-Flexi Periscoop!

Just what I was thinking, Amy!

Now we just had to find the bag.

But guess who
showed up to
block our way:

Zoe and her
meanie friends

Ideas were coming to me so fast I could barely

keep up with them. I gave Zoe my Diva-Pro

Ultra-Heated Hair Rollers to distract her.

She didn't know whether to fix her hair or carry

on being mean to me. Finally her hair won and

Amy and I were on our way again.

We ran outside and round to the Principal's office window to see if the F.P.B. was using it as a base.

Then we crouched down to make some important changes to The Super-Flexi Periscoop, using some wire, lots of duct tape and one of my super-strong magnets.

Invention 100:
(according to Dad, this one really will work!)
The New And Improved
Super-Flexi MAGNO-Periscoop

I peered through the window again. The bag was in full view. So was the F.P.B., who had now changed out of hiS disguise.

Yes, you read that right Edison ... the F.P.B./hairy horse lady wasn't a lady at all!

This is Mole 1. Operation nearly complete. Back to base at 1300 hours.

He was talking into his watch.

We had to act fast, but I was worried The Super-Flexi Magno-Periscoop might not be long enough to reach into the bag and pick up the ribbon.

I told Amy to hold on to my legs.

I was going in!

I was hardly breathing as I found myself looking down on Mole 1. While he was fiddling with his spy-watch, I started to lower the magnet towards the bag.

Closer ... closer ... CLOSER ...

But then Mole 1 bent over the bag! And before I could stop it the super-strong magnet had attached itself to his belt.

He started to spin around and around, trying to see what he was attached to. I held on tight to The Super-Flexi Magno-Periscoop, but I could feel the wire unravelling more and more, and Amy's hands were almost slipping off my ankles ...

Aaaarghhhhhhhhh!

The next thing we knew, I'd fallen into the room and brought Amy with me.

But when we stood up we saw something amazing.

Mole 1 was completely tangled up in the wire from our Super-Flexi Magno-Periscoop!

I grabbed the ribbon out of the bag.

Then I did something that felt just as good:
I hugged my brilliant assistant (and new human
best friend!), Amy.

Just as we were securing Mole 1, the door was kicked in.

And I couldn't believe who came rushing in ...

... Alice, Dad, Plum ... and Einstein!

Edison, I'll give you a moment to let all of that sink in.

Alright, that's long enough. I have so much more to tell you!

Alice stepped forward and took the ribbon from my hands and put it in her pocket.

Nice work, Eliza. As if finding the spy ribbon wasn't enough, you caught a dangerous enemy spy. His team have been trying to get their hands on this information for years.

I couldn't understand it. Alice usually says things like: "Go to bed, Eliza," and "Eat your peas, Eliza."

How did she know about this spy stuff?

Then she shook my hand and said something
even more strange.

Senior Agent Electra at your service.
I'm pleased to inform you that your
100th invention has just saved
Mission Metallic!

I can't remember exactly what I said but I think
it was something like:

HUH?

I asked Dad how they'd tracked me — and the ribbon — to Principal Bixley's office.

It was Einstein!
He buried my missing tracking device for the spy ribbon in his special burying place — where I found everything else he's buried. The tracking device led us here!

Good dog!

I told you he was a genius!

Alice, A.K.A. Senior Agent Electra, put her arm around me.

You did a great job, Eliza. I'll explain everything when we get home.

And home is where I am right now, Edison. Amy's here too, for a sleepover, and she's even brought her dog.

Amy's dog, Luna

I'd better go. I'll explain more tomorrow.

Yours triumphantly,
Eliza Boom
Assistant Inventor and Enemy Spy-Capturer!

P.S. Alice is still my step-mum. She just leads a double life. She and Dad work together, and She (Alice) was the shadowy figure I saw on the computer screen in Dad's shed/lab.

AWESOME!

lice, step-mum

Alice, A.K.A. Spy Boss

FRIDAY MORNING
My Lab, 7am

Dear Edison,

Six brilliant things:

1. Dad's job is safe.

Dad's happy thoughts!

Eliza saved the day!

My genius MindReader2000 reads minds again, YES!!

I want pancakes for breakfast.

2. Alice said she wanted to show me something special. But when she took me to her prize rose bush I was disappointed. I was about to explain how boring gardening is when ...

Best rose bush EVER!

... a trap door opened up and Alice led me to her secret underground spy HQ!

I bet Zoe Wakefield hasn't got one of these!

Things could not get better than that ... oh, wait, they could!

Brilliant thing number 3 is that school is closed for a little holiday.

Yesterday, Amy remembered that all the teachers were locked up, and we went back to rescue them.

We can't go back to school until the security has been investigated.

My school, CLOSED!

That could take weeks! Which means more time for my inventions, including ...

... brilliant thing number 4: Egg-Away Shampoo.

Invention 101

I invented a special shampoo for Amy.

To be honest, I don't think she ever really smelled that badly of eggs but as long as she's happy, I'm happy.

Now for brilliant thing number 5:
I've been promoted!

Senior Agent Electra says I have great potential.
She still won't tell me what secret info is on the
spy ribbon, but all in good time, Edison.

Best family EVER!

Amy's just woken up and we're going to invent something amazing for breakfast.

Invention 102 ... maybe?

Egg
Mushrooms
Bacon
Sausages
Beans

See you soon, Edison!

Yours inventively

(for ever!),
Eliza Boom
Best Friend
Dog-Lover
Assistant Inventor
and Junior Spy

P.S. I almost forgot!

Brilliant thing number 6.

Zoe Wakefield's hair after she'd used my
Diva-Pro Ultra-Heated Hair Rollers ...

... BOOM!

Grab your copy of Eliza
Boom's next adventure!

Out now!

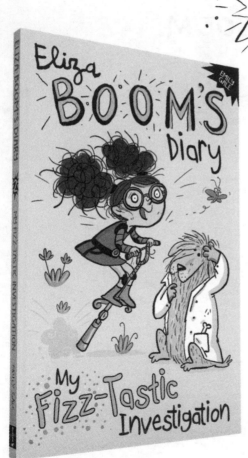

978-1-78055-241-5